Right Off 95

Anthony Hilliard Jr

ISBN: 979-8-218-93921-2

DEDICATION

I'd like to dedicate this book to all the people I've had the privilege to know and love but sadly aren't here in the physical. Their spirit and influence is still felt and appreciated.

Derrick "Sick -L" Liles
Ronnie Webb Jr
Mrs Pearl Williams
Anthony Hilliard Sr
Jerry "PaPa" Pender
Bessie "Ma Bet" Farmer
John" Mr Jack" Farmer
Kedron "Bless" Walker
Latoya Murphy
Aaliyah Qaadir
Maine McCall
Jermaine Moore
Monta Grace Hilliard
Desmond "Panama Gat" Williams

Disclaimer

This work is inspired by real events. Some names, characters, locations, and identifying details have been changed or altered to protect the privacy of individuals. Any resemblance to actual persons, living or deceased, is coincidental or used fictitiously.

PREFACE

The most basic explanation for life I've found has been a circle. A circle can be interpreted as a continuum or a never-ending loop. I was taught early about how things go from ashes to ashes, dust to dust. If you do good, good will come to you, or if you do bad, then bad is coming. No matter if you use religion, different cultures, or even science, it all comes back to a circle. "Energy can't be created or destroyed," "For every action, there is an equal or greater reaction," etc. I'm sure you get the point.

As a youth, you don't ponder the repercussions of your actions as heavily as you would in adulthood. Thank God for praying grandmothers and mothers. If you grew up in the 80s and 90s, the drug culture influence was so abundant that you could be submerged in it unknowingly. It was everywhere. So was popular music such as rap, movies, and even fashion. Certain cars that were desired could be traced back to your local drug dealer's tastes.

My mother did everything she possibly could to steer me clear of certain actions that could yield unfavorable reactions, but again, the influence was heavy. When you mix all of that with young adult invincibility theories and boldness, you end up with interesting recipes. As wild as this personal story reads, it's actually about 95% true. Whether I went through it personally or told someone else's story, this is a solid recounting of events.

This is a unique yet relatable testimony meant to heal and possibly influence others to pay close attention to what they consume and also to take close consideration of certain choices that may be pivotal.

I thought this story was my story for years, but it's actually our story. That is, if you grew up in the 90s, "Right Off 95."

CONTENTS

ACKNOWLEDGMENTS

Special thanks to:

Paulette Hilliard
Annette Hilliard
Shameka Hilliard
Tnitra King
Tanisha Roberts
Daria Miller
Candice Braswell
Jon Mullins
Ali Goins
Antonio Mendez
Dr James "Limitless" Williams
Michael Dew
Anthony Bynum
Errol Frails
Shemeka Valencia
Juwon Cosey
Jayvin Finch
Teresa Ledgester
Uddy Bullock

SCENE 1: NICKS WENT FOR 20s DOWN SOUTH

Somewhere in New York, a gold Nissan Maxima is parked in front of what looks like an abandoned building. The car is idling while Eric B and Rakim's "Mahogany" plays low in the background. Inside the cupholder lies half a 40 oz of Old English in a paper bag and an ashtray full of cigarette butts and weed roaches.

Driver:
I'm telling you, B, it's too many hustlers in the city and not enough fiends, nicca. We sitting on six bricks and a couple pounds of lime. No movement, just sitting.

The passenger, Benny, replies.

Benny:
Don't worry. I got an idea about how to make these dollars make sense. All this time, I'm out here breaking my neck, breaking day tryna outhustle the next nicca, not seeing clearly. See, I gotta work smarter, not harder. It's simple business, supply and demand. It's hella supply out here but not enough demand, so I gotta find some more customers or take some niccas off this earth, but the city too flooded for that. Take one huster out, two mo pop up. Plus, when bodies pile up, shit is bad for business anyway.

Driver:
So what you saying, Benny? All this business talk sound like some White people shit.

Benny:
I'm saying it's time to relocate. We right here at the ports, so we get it low. But everybody gets it low, so we need to head away from the city down I-95 and get this paper from these country bama muthafuckas. Them niccas slow down there. I can flood the city and cash out before niccas knew I was even there. I got family in the Carolinas, so I'mma go down and peep shit. The holidays coming up, so it's the perfect time.

Driver:
That's brilliant, my nicca. We gon be paid on some Scarface mob shit. How Biggie say that shit? "Nicks went for twenty down south."

They both laugh.

Driver:
Ok, that's cool. When we leaving? I need to pack and holla at my BM and tell her I'm sliding for a little bit. In the meantime, I'mma take half this weight to the stash. When you called and told me to bring the bricks, I thought you had a sale or something right now, but that's even better, my nicca.

Benny:
See, that's the thing... I do need them right now.

Before the driver can say another word, Benny pulls the blade out of his leather Avirex jacket, covers the driver's mouth, and stabs him quickly three times to the abdominal region and holds it on the last poke, twisting and turning it like he is carving his name into the driver's body.

As the last bit of life escapes the driver's body, Benny leans over to look him in the eyes and whispers.

Benny:
Nothing personal, nicca. I just decided to dissolve our partnership in order to pursue my own interests. And for the record, that ain't no White people shit, B... It's just business.

Benny carefully wipes down everything in the car and grabs the weight and Old English. He takes a gas can he had hidden by a trash can and soaks the car with gasoline. Just as he lights a match, he pauses, blows out the match, opens the car door, and presses eject on the CD player to grab the Eric B and Rakim CD. He then lights another match, ignites the inferno, and dashes off from the crime scene.

NEW YORK
8CT-9483

SCENE 2: GHOSTRIDE THE WHIP

As the sun starts to go down on a small town in North Carolina, there lies a row of cars parked next to the curb illegally on purpose. The sounds of Mase's Harlem World blasting from a small hatchback car sets the mood for this young adult gathering.

Next to the car stands a smooth brother clean cut from his burgundy Avirex jacket to his matching burgundy timbs with a low fade and Versace link chain. He is different from the other young men mainly because he embodies the same music he's playing out of his car. He is actually from Harlem, NY, undeniably, thus the nickname "Harlem."

Harlem shouts to the group of guys rolling dice near the curb.

Harlem:
Hurry up, Dee, and win my money back. Maverick had me down $200.

Tightly parked against the curb lay a green Honda Accord directly behind the hatchback. This car belongs to Dee. As cold as it is, Dee has his jacket on top of the car as he rolls dice with Maverick and Webber, sweating like he is running full court. He really enjoyed gambling; it was like a sport to him. The rush always had him feeling like he was unbeatable, almost like he was in Vegas up a $100,000 or something. Whether it was playing cards, rolling dice, pitching quarters, or popping pencils, Dee wanted in.

Dee:
I gotcha, Harlem. "Daddy need some new shoes!"

Webber:
Daddy 'bout to be barefooted if you keep rolling how you rolling nicca.

Dee rolls the dice and catches 7.

Maverick:
FUCK!

Webber:
Man, this some bullshit!

Dee:
Thank you, my kind sirs. You just paid for my next pair of Buttas.

They all laugh.

Suddenly, a Black Toyota Celica, followed by a white Ford Explorer, creeps down the block, each of the vehicles being driven by their owners who are sitting on the hoods and windshields of the vehicles. The skinny young man with the North Carolina A and T sweater is riding on the windshield of the Toyota with his hand sticking through the sunroof steering the car, while the athletically built guy in all fatigue BDU's is steering his truck through the driver window. Undoubtedly, this dangerous show-off move was learned from watching too much TV. They called it "ghostriding the whip."

They parked directly behind the other cars on the block and greeted their friends.

Harlem: (yells out to the Celica driver)
Yo, Vega, that was alright, but I see you almost lost it at the end trying to be me.

Vega:
You wish, nicca. You just mad 'cause you New York niccas swear you the best drivers because y'all be stealing cars and shit.

Harlem:
Wrong state, asshole. I told you to quit watching New Jersey Drive.

Dee:
Vega, How you and Dome pull up at the same time? I thought you weren't coming home till later from school break. Shit, we knew Dome's ass would be back soon as he could.

Webber:
That nicca Dome tired of eating them rations and potatoes or whatever universal soldiers eat.

They all laugh and continue to joke and play as more of their friends and girls pull up. Being that small towns don't have much to do for youth, it's very common to pick a spot and post up to create your own fun and genuinely enjoy each other's company. And idle time makes it equally easy to get into mischief.

NC A&T
6ALCB37

SCENE 3: COUNTRY COUSINS

Benny slows down on I-95 South and takes an exit into a small town in North Carolina. He travels through the small city, surprised at the new businesses. Things are slightly different than how he remembers, but the distinct smell of pigs and tobacco is unforgettable. He frowns in disgust from the stench as he makes a right off the street to turn down a dirt path. As he pulls closer to the double-wide trailer, a pitbull circles his car. He then spots a heavy-set older woman with grey hair sitting at a picnic table in front of the trailer, smoking a cigarette.

Lady:
Nephew! Look at you looking just like yo daddy. I swear it's like he spat you right out. Come get out that car and give yo aunt a hug with yo handsome self.

Benny:
Hey Aunt Linda, I will! soon as you tie that werewolf up somewhere.

Linda:
Hush, boy. That dog ain't gon bother you. Most he gon do is lick you to death. The neighbor cat chased that dog clean cross town. Had me looking that mut for 'bout two days.

Benny hugs his Aunt Linda.

Linda:
Boy, I missed you so much. I wish my brother was alive to see his twin.

A tear falls from Linda's cheek as she embraces Benny even tighter.

Linda:
It makes me so mad to think 'bout how them folks treated him in that prison. That was no way for nobody to go.

Benny:
It's alright, Auntie. I made peace with that a long time ago. I'm good, trust me. You ain't gotta worry 'bout me.

Linda:
I'm worried looking at cha right now because you look like you hungry. They don't feed you up there, Benjamin Jr.

Benny:
Chill, Auntie. Don't nobody call me that.

Linda:
Boy, hush and grab yo bags. Yo cousin in there still sleep with his lazy ass. I know he gon be surprised to see you. Plus, I got some turkey wings and collards in there. I'mma fix you a plate right quick.

They walk into the trailer, and Linda goes immediately into the kitchen to wash her hands and prepare the plate. Dionne Warrick's "Deja Vu" is playing from an old record player in the living room.

Linda:
Go back to the back room and wake yo cousin up. He needs to be up anyway. That lazy rascal. It's two beds in there, so make yourself right at home, baby. I'll have yo plate ready in 'bout five minutes.

She yells, "Nate, get yo ass up we got company!"

Benny walks back to the room, bag in hand. As soon as he opens the door, Nate rushes him and starts wrestling him playfully. They tussle for a little bit and bump into the wall as Benny starts to get the best of Nate.

Linda: (yelling)
I know you niccas ain't wrestling in my house like 12-year-olds. You done lost yo goddamn minds. Cut it out before I shoot both you fools!

They stop tussling and embrace in a hug.

Nate:
You know she ain't playing, right? She a shooter like yo daddy.

Benny:
I remember. Aunt Linda ain't never play. I remember she kept a .38 with the tape on the handle.

Nate:
That's the gun she talking 'bout.

They both laugh hysterically.

Nate:
I miss you, cuz. Jr., it's good to see you. Why you don't visit as much?

Benny:
To tell you the truth, B, it was a little hard after Pops passed. I really just been on my own grind, being my own man. I'mma get this paper how I get it so I can live like a king.

Nate:
I feel that, cuzzo. Speaking of that, I know you brought some of that good down with you. Fire up, nicca.

Benny:
You already know family. Matter of fact, after I eat this plate, we can smoke and talk.

Nate:
Bet, you know you gotta eat that whole plate or Mom's gonna shoot you with that rusty ass gun.

They both laugh as Benny walks to the kitchen to sit down and eat.

Benny follows Nate out of the trailer and yells back to Linda.

Benny:
Thank you, Auntie. That bird was everything.

Nate:
Roll up, nicca.

Nate hands Benny rolling papers.

Benny laughs.

Benny:
Nah, nicca, we smoke white owls and Phillies up top, B. We ain't smoking no dirt ass reffa, nicca. This that lime mixed with that chocolate. I already had one rolled up because I knew you'd want that high power.

Nate excitedly grabs the blunt, lights, and inhales. He starts coughing and choking immediately as the potent smoke enters his lungs.

Nate:
Damn, nicca. This shit serious. This ain't no regular weed. Ain't nothing around here like this.

Benny:
Nah, it ain't. But that's exactly why I wanted to come here and holla at you family. I got this all day, every day, B. I'mma flood the city with this green and white, straight takeover. You with me, cuzzo?

Nate:
You already know, fam. Say less.

SCENE 4: BROTHERS FROM ANOTHER

A clear, cool Saturday morning at about 11:00 am sits Vega, Dee, and Harlem on a green electric box. A black Chevy Tahoe with 20-inch rims pulls up to the curb, playing Group Home's "Suspended in Time." Vega rises up from the box and bops towards the truck, reciting the lyrics from the song.

Vega:
"Nowhere near simple. My mental, flex more complex than Mozart's instrumentals!"

A brown-skinned, chubby Black male rolls the passenger window down all the way so that he can extend his hand to Vega and dap him up. Vega immediately extends his arm and meets the greeting in a welcomed fashion.

Vega:
Wassup, Maine. How you?

Maine smiles and motions for his beautiful lady driver to turn the music down.

Maine:
"Vega, how u doin', my friend?" (playful Latino accent) You don't know nothing 'bout the Group Home.

Vega:
"I'm well, my friend" (equally playful Latino voice). Stop it. You know I love Gang Starr and anything Premo puts his touch to. Who's this lovely Latino friend you have driving for you?

Vega leans into the window and speaks Spanish.

Vega:
"*Eres una muchacha muy buenita.*" — You're a very sweet girl.

The female smiles as Vega winks. Maine playfully thumps Vega in the chest.

Maine:
"Hey, my friend, dats not cho' cheese" (Latino accent).

They all laugh.

Vega:
What's good, Maine? What you need?

Maine:
Let me get a quarter, fam. I got a room at the heart, so I'mma be on the low all day learning Spanish. You feel me?

Maine hands tightly folded money to Vega, and Vega slides money into his pocket on the low.

Vega:
Yea, I get it. I don't blame you. Ask her if she got a sister. I need some mo' lessons myself.

Vega looks back at Harlem and Dee and says, "QBC sip lime Bacardi." Harlem gets up and looks towards the end of the street, then rubs his hands together. A tall male in a hoodie whistles once from the other edge of the street.

Dee gets up from the box and walks to the back of the apartment building. He looks around, then grabs a Dorito bag from behind a trash can. He pulls an orange square plastic baggy from the Dorito bag and puts the bag back in place. He walks back around the building and strolls towards the Tahoe.

Dee:
Wuddup, Maine? I see you studying abroad.

Maine:
Yessir, mi amigo. Pass the green, por favor, negro.

Dee daps Maine at the same time exchanging product. Maine smiles and turns up the radio, motioning for his lady friend to drive off. Dee and Vega return to the green electric box.

A gold van comes down the street as the Tahoe pulls off, and it turns into the driveway opposite the green box. An older Black female opens the trunk and waves to the boys on the green box.

Dee:
Hey, Ma Bet. How you doing?

Vega and Harlem, in unison, repeat, "Hey, Ma Bet."

Ma Bet:
Hey, boys. Help me with these fishing rods and grab this bag. Y'all ate yet?

Ma Bet isn't really any of their mothers, but she is like the neighborhood mom. She treats all the boys like her sons, and her daughters are like their sisters. In the South, feeding someone is definitely a show of love.

Ma Bet:
I brought y'all boys some chicken from Parkers. Help yourself.

The boys: (in unison)
THANKS, MA BET!

SCENE 5: COUNTRY ASS BAMAS

Jay drives down the dirt road as a dog chases the car. He pulls in front of the trailer, playing Old Dirty Bastard's verse from "Da Mystery of Chessboxing." He hops out of the car and plays with the dog as the dog responds in a friendly manner. His music continues to blast as he quotes Method Man's part.

Linda comes out of the trailer.

Linda:
Boy, if you don't turn that music down, I'mma call Pearl and tell her she gon have to come bury you.

Jay:
My bad, Aunt Linda.

Jay turns the radio down.

Jay:
My mom told me to come bring you her homemade Pearl Babies candy.

Linda:
Yes! Well, I hope she sent two boxes this time. Last time she made some, yo cousin ate 'em before I could get right many of 'em. Him and Benny in the backyard right now.

Jay: (with a slight hesitation)
Benny? Like Jr? Uncle Benji son from New York?

Linda:
Yea, he down here visiting. Go round back. You act like you scared or sum'n. You know blood thicker than water.

Jay walks around back and sees Nate and Benny by the firepit in the backyard.

Nate:
Jay wassup, cuz? What you up to, you beige snapping turtle?

Jay:
Nothing, just bringing your mom some Pearl Babies, you shaved squirrel nutsack.

Benny:
Waddup, lil cuz, how you? I see you got some height on you, B. You feel like you can beat me now? Huh?

Benny looks at Jay with a serious expression. Nate and Jay get quiet.

Benny laughs.

Benny:
You know I'm just fucking with you right, nicca?

Jay and Nate laugh along partially.

Benny:
How Ms. Pearl and your little brother? Fam good?

Jay:
Yea, everybody good. How long you been home?

Benny:
I just got here, maybe a day or two. Thought I'd spend the holidays with you country muthafuckas. Nate been showing me around. Shit looks wild and different since I left. I don't recognize none of these new roads and people.

Jay:
I know what you do recognize tho.

Jay: (pointing to the blunt in his hand)
Let me hit that. I smelled that walking back here. Nate got you back here smoking that dookie he be getting from Saratoga?

Nate:
Shut up, Jay. That aint my shit. Why you talking, you mouthy slow tapeworm?

Benny:
Hit this, cuzzo. You tell me.

Jay grabs the blunt and inspects it for a second.

Jay:
Well, I know Nate ain't roll this. This shit look aero dye nammiick.

They all laugh at Jay's mispronunciation of his expression.

Then Jay takes a puff of the blunt and coughs almost immediately.

Jay:
Goddamn!

Jay coughs more intensely, tears coming to his eyes as Nate and Benny laugh at him.

Jay:
What the…(coughs) fuck is… (coughs) this?

Benny:
This that Harlem world shit, little cousin, and I got plenty mo, nicca. I'm 'bout to flood this city. Since you fam, I'mma look out.

Jay passes the blunt to Nate and coughs once more but gathers himself.

Jay:
I know a couple people I can turn you onto because this some Phi-yah!

Benny smiles.

Benny:
Talk to me, cousin.

SCENE 6: BLOW THE CARTRIDGE

GZA's "Liquid Swords" plays loud through Jay and Maverick's dad's house speakers while Dee, Harlem, Rob, Dome, and Vega are playing an intense game of Golden Eye on Nintendo. Jay walks into the room, dipping a cracker into a can of potted meat.

Harlem:
Jay, I don't see how the fuck you eat that crazy shit. You eating straight cat food, B.

Jay smiles immediately and continues eating out of his can. He then mumbles while he eats.

Jay:
Dis shit good. You want some?

Vega:
I ain't gon front, it's alright with a little bit of hot sauce. I used to trade Jay Nintendo games for cans of potted meat or Vienna.

Rob:
It do look like cat food. That's why Jay over there smiling like he got whiskers.

Dee:
He smiles like that anyway. Y'all need to pay attention to this game. Who running around with that midget Oddjob killing everybody with that grenade launcher?

Dee's phone rings, and he hands Rob the controller and steps away.

Dee answers. He has a small conversation to the side, walks back frustrated, and motions to Rob to get the controller back.

Rob:
Dee, I'm killing 'em. Let me finish Vega off. I got 'em running.

Dee:
Go ahead, you good.

Dee sits on the couch, still frustrated.

Harlem:
What's wrong? You look like you just broke up with Kia or sum'n. I told you, you gotta have options. I'll teach you how to stay on this fly shit.

Dee:
Nah, nicca. I just got a call that I can't re-up. I need some green ASAP before niccas end up going somewhere else. It's dry everywhere.

Jay:
I got a cousin from up top that got some fire.

Dee:
Nicca, when was you gon tell somebody?

Dome:
Jay sitting around here with connects on reefa not saying nothing.

Jay:
I ain't really know about it. He my cousin, but I don't really fuck with him like that, and he stay in NY. I just happened to go visit my Aunt Linda, and him and Nate was out back smoking.

Vega:
Fuck that. If he got green we should cop, especially if them prices right.

Dee:
Call him, Jay. Ask him can we see something.

Jay calls his cousin, and about 26 minutes later, a car pulls in front of the house playing Kool G Rap's "It's a Shame." The car turns off, and Benny hops out in a pair of Vasque gore-tex boots, Guess jeans, a Sergio Tacchini collar polo, and an aviator jacket.

Jay meets Benny at the door and leans in to greet him. The boys continue playing the game as Jay, Benny, Vega, and Dee walk through the living room to Jay's bedroom.

Jay stands between everyone.

Jay:
Wassup, cuz? These my boys, Vega and Dee. They the ones that was asking to see something.

Benny pulls out an ounce of lime-green weed that you can smell before he even opens the bag.

Dee:
Damn, that shit smell good. I already know I'mma need this ounce for dolo and at least a QP.

Benny:
I got whatever you need. This just a small taste tho. I got white, soft, hard, whatever, B.

Vega grabs the ounce from Dee and inspects the product. He noticed the elegant crystals and beautiful fine hairs. They are like bright orange highlights speckled throughout the lime-green soft texture, definitely something you'd see in High Times magazine.

Dee:
How much for the QP?

Benny:
$175 for y'all, but anybody else, $250.

Dee pulls out a wallet with a naked lady on it immediately and starts counting money. Vega and Benny lock eyes for a moment, and Vega puts his hand out, blocking Dee.

Vega:
We good.

Dee:
What you mean?

Benny looks puzzled and slightly angry as Vega grabs the ounce that Jay is now holding and hands it back to Benny

Vega:
We good right now, but we'll hit you if we need something.

Dee looks puzzled but trusts Vega and agrees.

Benny looks at Jay as if he wants to explode for having a group of kids wasting his time. Benny turns to Vega and smiles.

Benny: (calmly)
Bet. Yo, Jay, let me holla at you real quick, B.

Jay follows Benny through the living room, past the boys playing the game, and enters Jay's parents' bathroom. As Jay steps into the bathroom, Benny closes the door behind them, pulls a Chrome .357 out of the back of his waist, and aims it directly at Jay's nose.

Benny:
Don't you ever waste my time again, cuz. I've shot muthafuckas over less. Ain't nobody playing and doing takebacks out here, nicca. Fuck you think this is?!

Jay pushes the .357 out his face, calling his bluff.

Jay:
Get that shit out my face.

Benny laughs.

Benny:
You lucky you family and it's a whole house full of witnesses. I ain't bring enough bullets to body you and all your friends.

Jay stares in angry silence as Benny puts the gun back into the small of his back.

Benny smiles and then opens the door. He then heads out the front door, hops in his car, and drives away.

Jay exits the bathroom and goes to sit on the couch quietly by himself. Dee and Vega still remain in Jay's room.

Dee:
Yo, what the fuck? Why you ain't let me cop? That weed look like some shit Snoop Dogg be smoking on.

Vega quickly makes up a lie because he is afraid of how his feelings will be dismissed. Something about Benny just didn't sit right with his spirit, and Vega comes from a long line of discerners that trust what most call a gut feeling, aka holy spirit.

Vega:
Trust me, that weed ain't look right. It was too good to be true. We don't know him. You know how some of them niccas up top be trying to fool us. Then you would have been out of your money and stuck with some fa-gazey.

Dee:
Stuck? I woulda sold all that shit, stems, seeds, and all.

They both laugh and head back into the living room to play the game with the others when they notice Jay on the couch to himself.

Vega:
Jay, you good? You ok?

Jay:
Yea, I'm straight, just waiting for my turn on the game.

Vega:
Alright, cool. I got next after Jay.

SCENE 7: BLOWING OFF STEAM

Benny pulls into a set of projects called The Chapel. He parks the car and pops his trunk. He looks around for cops and nosey neighbors, pulls a green JanSport book bag out of the car, and proceeds to go upstairs to the first apartment on the right. He knocks on the door—three knocks, a pause, and two more knocks. A female voice responds.

Female:
Who dat?

Benny:
Benny! Now open the fucking door.

A thick, tall, voluptuous redbone with a short blonde cut looking like Eve from Ruff Ryders opens the door. She is gorgeous and talks naturally in a sweet, subtle tone like a phone sex operator. A gold nameplate necklace that reads "Toya" lays on her fitted baby doll top with no bra over her small but erect bee stings. She opens the door, and Benny walks in.

Female:
Damn, nicca. Fuck is wrong with you? I'm just doing what you said to do, following orders and shit.

Benny walks past her and proceeds to the kitchen. He opens the JanSport bag and puts a few ounces of weed and a quarter-brick of white on the table. He opens the wrapped cocaine and takes out enough for personal use, then hands the drugs to Toya. Toya takes the drugs and disappears into the back room to the stash.

Benny makes two lines of coke on a pink hand mirror that is lying on the kitchen table. Toya returns to the kitchen as Benny takes the first sniff and leans back in the chair. He then wipes his nose and puts his left hand in his pants to grab his dick.

Toya grabs Benny's arm, pulls his hands out of his pants, and straddles him.

Toya:
You lucky I love your fine ass. Come in here all frazzled and angry like a stereotypical New York drug dealer. Why you more wound up than usual?

Benny:
Ain't nothin'. Just some bullshit kids I shoulda gave some act right. Little niccas think it's a game out here. My cousin Jay lucky he fam 'cause ain't got no problem bodying anybody.

Toya leans in closer, starts kissing Benny's neck.

Toya: (whispering)
Baby, I know you come from a long line of niccas you don't play with. I remember hearing stories about your father and uncles. Anybody that know know. No question, you the realest nicca I ever met. And that makes you even sexier. Just promise me you'll be careful out there. Can't have your story end the same way as the one you told me about your father. Generational curses are real.

Benny:
I ain't my father! You…my aunt… EVERYBODY! act like I'm gonna end up like that nicca. At least up top, I ain't gotta hear this same bullshit all the time. You fucking stressing me, Toya.

Toya:
Baby, I'm sorry, you're right. You're right. You're not your father. But you do give me all that daddy dick.

Benny:
Bitch, you crazy.

Toya:
"You like that shit B." (NY accent)

Toya and Benny laugh.

Toya:
Just don't forget me come Christmas with all this love you getting down south. Your aunt still cooking for Christmas? Because it's been a minute since I had her stuffing. You know she used to feed the whole hood.

Benny:
Yea, she definitely cooking, and just believe you gon have to eat everything on your plate if you come.

Toya:
I can eat, nicca. We eat down south. You up north niccas be getting all skinny eating tofu and shit at the bodega. I'll probably eat more than you.

Benny looks into Toya's eyes and licks his lips.

Benny:
I always finish my plate.

Toya leans in to kiss Benny. While kissing and licking his lips, she loosens his belt and reaches to grab his throbbing member. Benny grabs her by the throat, and she lets out a moan immediately.

He then reaches with his other hand behind him to grab his hidden gun and place it on the table. The gun makes a hard thud as he proceeds to expose Toya's beautiful honey-brown breast.

He then pulls her nipple into his mouth aggressively as her head flings back, mouth open, allowing a deep, sultry moan to escape.

He picks her up, passionately kissing her, carrying her into the back room.

SCENE 8: CHRISTMAS ON THE DRIVE

Even though most of the boys scattered when they graduated, Christmas is one of those holidays where everyone comes home to visit family.

It was like a neighborhood reunion. There are about eight cars parked in a line on the dark street that they claimed proudly, Snowden Drive. The streetlights illuminate their paths. Lined in the middle of the street are young men in racing stances—Jay, Dee, Dash, Cole, Smaboo, Goodys, Dome, Maverick, Vega, Ghost, Webber, and Rob. Tko, Puff, and Pone were at the other end of the street, about 60 meters away, with their hands out, ready to verify the winner. Harlem watches, leaning against his car.

Tko:
Hurry up before a car comes.

Goodys:
Dee keeps cheating, edging up.

Cole:
Back up, Dee. Quit cheating.

Dee:
Ain't nobody cheating.These niccas scared.

Puff:
It ain't gon matter. Dome gon beat y'all. You know he on steroids.

Tko:
ON YOUR MARK…Get set…GOOOO!

They take off, and Cole slips and grabs Smaboo, laughing but also inadvertently tripping up Jay and Maverick. Dee catches a cramp mid-stride and stops while Vega, Ghost, Dash, Webber, and Rob get a good start but end up racing for third place. It's clear the real race is between the active army members Goodys and Dome. Although Goodys and Dome are neck-to-neck, Dome lets out his signature laugh and nudges past Goodys at the last minute.

Puff, Pone, and Tko yell simultaneously, "DOMEEEEEE!"

Goodys: (breathing heavily)
That nicca cheated with that laugh!

All the boys laugh hysterically.

Dash:
You know that's his afterburner.

Pone:
I don't know why y'all racing anyway. You know we all getting old.

Rob:
Speak for yourself. I'm still young and handsome. That's why Harlem's mom keep asking me to come over and screw in lightbulbs when he ain't home.

Harlem:
Quit talking 'bout my mom, dumb ass.

Vega:
You know your mom fine. I'm thinking 'bout filling out an application to be your daddy.

Harlem:
Nicca, I'm your daddy. Matter of fact, I'mma remember these momma jokes next time you need me to fix something.

Vega rushes Harlem playfully and hugs him.

Vega:
I'm just playing, Daddy. Please love me. Why have you forsaken me?

As the boys laugh, Harlem fights Vega's play hug, prying him off.

Harlem:
Nah, nicca, get off me, get off me. You can make it up to me by hooking me up with your cousin tho.

The boys all laugh and head inside Jay and Maverick's house.

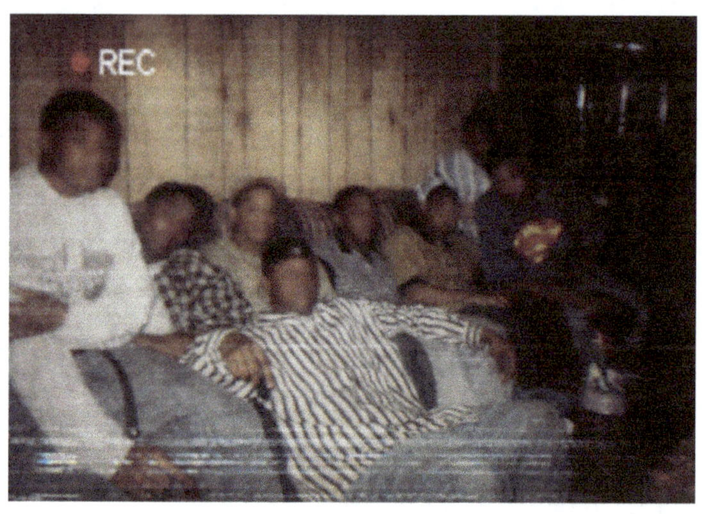
REC

SCENE 9: THE HAPPY STORE

All the boys go into the house while Jay and Vega lag a little behind the rest of the boys. Jay suddenly stops.

Jay:
Yo, Vega, can you run me to The Happy Store real quick?

Vega:
It's Christmas dude. How you even know they gon be open? What you need from the store?

Jay:
I'm hungry. I just want a hotdog and a honey bun.

Vega:
Nicca, you can't eat no leftovers. I know yo people cooked, plus how you even know the store open?

Jay:
Ain't no leftovers. Me and Maverick done kilt them. I went earlier. They open and the Black Presto, but you know they hot dogs fell off.

Vega:
Alright, nicca. Come on, but you buying me a yoohoo and a Swiss roll.

Jay and Vega hop into Vega's car and head to the store. When they get close, they see that the store is indeed open, and there are a few cars parked at the gas pumps and two more pulling into the parking lot. Jay points with excitement.

Jay:
See, I told you they was open.

Vega pulls into the opposite side of the store and parks. Jay excitedly hops out of the car before Vega can shut the engine off. As he's opening the door, he simultaneously closes the door without pause and rushes into the store.

Vega yells out the window.

Vega:
Damn, nicca quit slammin' Cadillac doors. Them hotdogs ain't going nowhere. You probably the only one that eats them shits, anyway. You gon fuck around and have bubble guts for Christmas.

Vega shuts off the engine and follows behind Jay. As Vega enters the store, he laughs to himself as he watches Jay prepare his hot dogs on the aisle. Vega goes to the cooler and grabs a chocolate yoohoo, then walks to the cash register and grabs a Swiss roll from the wall of snacks directly in front of the cashier.

Vega puts his drink and snack on the counter, slightly close to the cashier, and speaks.

Vega:
Pardon me, but my hungry friend is gonna pay for this for me as soon as he finish microwaving his hot dogs.

The cashier laughs and puts the items to the side. Suddenly, the store door swings open, and four young men enter. One of them spots Jay on the aisle and taps his homeboy, and they both smile and head straight to Jay. Before Jay or Vega notice the approach, the light-skinned, shorter guy walks up to Jay, gets uncomfortably close, and begins to yell at Jay.

Light-skinned Guy:
I heard you going around telling niccas you beat my ass the other week.

Jay's posture indicates that he's taken off guard and possibly afraid, but he manages to get up the courage to reply.

Jay:
Keith, I ain't say nothing. What's done is done. I ain't got no mo' problems with you.

As the disagreement ensues, Vega rushes over to get in between his friend and Keith. The other men are standing closely around Keith but wait patiently in anticipation of any kind of action.

Vega:
Chill, Keith, it's Christmas. Ain't nobody trying to do nothing. We should all just go home. Can we do this another day?

Keith:
Fuck that! This nicca run his mouth too much.

Keith tries to get closer to Jay, but Vega steps in between the advancement.

Vega:
Come on, Keith. Jay said he ain't got no more issues with you. It's Christmas, dude!

Keith:
Nicca, I don't give a fuck about Christmas, and fuck you!

Vega's facial expression changes as he pulls off his jacket and lays it across the candy aisle and then faces Keith eye to eye.

Vega:
Nicca, I tried to leave, but I ain't gon beg. I ain't Jay. What's up!

Keith backs up a little bit, and it's complete silence until a tall, skinny, dark-skinned guy with dreads yells out from behind him.

Tall Dark-skinned Guy:
Fuck that, Keith! Hit that nicca.

Vega:
Nicca, shut the fuck up. You can get it too. I'm done talking. Any of y'all can get it!

The tall guy edges closer, and Vega swings a violent haymaker, just missing the guy's head but hitting the beverage door cooler. The guy rushes forward, wrestling Vega as they barrel into the corner of the chips aisle, knocking over a display full of different flavored Doritos. As they continue to tussle, Vega feels his opponent starting to get the best of him as he begins to lift off his feet. Thinking quickly, Vega manages to secure a headlock in order to stop the ascension and prevent what would surely be a WWF slam on his head.

Vega then squeezed the headlock as tight as he could in order to cut off the oxygen supply of the stronger fighter. The quick decision works, and Vega feels his feet plant back on earth. Vega realizes a wrestling match with the taller, stronger opponent would probably ensure an L, so he releases the headlock and throws a fierce combination, frustrating the dreaded fellow. The dreaded guy rushes Vega again as Vega sidesteps, grabs a handful of his dreads, and uppercuts him with his free hand repeatedly as the guy yells out.

Tall Dark-skinned Guy:
Keith, help. He got my dreads!

Keith rushes over and swings, catching Vega with a sucker punch and forcing him to release the guy's dreads as they both hit the floor. Jay hits Keith, and Keith and Jay rumble, bursting through the store door, followed by two other guys. Slightly disoriented, Vega bounces back up immediately and grabs Heineken bottles, pitching them like an MLB player at anyone he sees. Bottles explode against aisles and windows as his enemies flee out the door on the opposite side of the store, yelling.

Vega rushes out the door to help Jay up, only to find Jay brushing himself off while police cars approach. They both run back through the store to the opposite door, hop in Vega's car, and speed off, narrowly escaping police.

While Vega's adrenaline is still pumping, he yells out, speeding down the 301 highway.

Vega:
Fuck them niccas! I want Keith! That nicca wanna hit me when I was fucking his homeboy up! I'll kill them muthafuckas! I can't wait to get my hands on both dem dumb as niccas!

Jay:
The one you fought name Slug. Me and Maverick fought them last weekend. All they do is fight.

Vega:
I got what they looking for. I need 'em both one-on-one, or we can get into some wild shit with the boys. Hands, guns, I don't give a FUCK!

Jay:
I'm with you. It's whatever!

Two more cops speed past the boys on the highway with blue lights flashing.

Jay:
Quick, take the back way to the crib before they try and pull us.

Vega turns on a back street and speeds towards their destination. A few moments later, they pull up at Jay's house, park, and rush into the house. They storm inside, still frantic bouncing off the wall as Dee catches sight of them first.

Dee:
What the fuck is wrong with y'all?

Jay: (yells out while holding his ribs)
We just fought Keith and Slug at The Happy Store!

Maverick:
What the fuck? Let's go back!

Vega:
I don't think they still there. We bounced. We had to get out of there before the cops pulled up.

Maverick:
I just beat that nicca ass last weekend. Now he wanna fuck with my brother. I'mma kill me a nicca.

Jay: (shushing)
Hey, let's step outside. My dad gon get mad if we keep yelling.

All the boys go outside and sit on and around the green electric box.

Rob:
Why y'all go to the store anyway? It's Christmas. I ain't think The Happy Store was open.

Vega:
This nicca wanted a hot dog and a honey bun.

Dash:
Why? Y'all ain't just eat leftovers?

Vega:
That's what I said.

They all laugh.

Dee:
I think Slug stay off Gold Street. We can go by there, plus you know they gon be at the Christmas tournament.

Vega:
Hell yea. We can't really do it inside the gym because the cops will probably break it up and catch us. We can run up on them outside, that way we can fuck them up, then hop in the cars and jet.

Harlem:
Good idea. I'm with that too.

Vega:
That's what it is. Everybody, bring your burners just in case, but hopefully, we can keep this shit on some one-on-one shit because they not deep as us. That shit will be a slaughter if they even think about doing something dumb.

Jay:
Bet let's link on the drive tomorrow 'bout 5.

All of the boys agree unanimously, shaking hands and exchanging customary dap, saying their goodbyes for the night.

SCENE 10: LIKE FATHER LIKE SON

Three days after Christmas, Benny, Nate, and Toya are sitting at a small table at Aunt Linda's trailer. 2pac's "If My Homies Call" is playing through Benny's car window, parked not too far from the table. Nate begins to pour three more shots for each of them from a half-full gallon jug of apple pie-flavored corn liquor. Benny reaches over the table and grabs Nate's chain in admiration.

Benny:
Damn cousin, your chain kinda nice, B. That Jesus piece chunky. Let me hold sum'n.

Benny and Nate laugh.

Nate:
You like that? Keep making us rich, and I'mma fuck around and go cop a Cuban like your dad had back in the day.

Benny's facial expression changes.

Toya:
Why you have to go and mention his dad? Dumb ass.

Nate:
I ain't mean nothing by it. He know his daddy was a fly-ass gangsta. We gon run this city just like he did.

Benny:
It's alright, Toya. That shit don't even phaze me no more. I'm so used to this around here. It's always gonna be "Your daddy this, your daddy that." This my roots. I know his blood pump through me, but I'm a whole other animal. You feel me, B? I'm a fucking money-making fly-ass monster out here. My name gon ring out like Scarface.

Toya:
I hear all that, nicca, but why you babysitting that shot? What's wrong? You scared of this good ol' corn?

Benny:
Fuck outta here. They don't make a bottle or stupid jug I can't make it to the bottom of. Let me show you how we do it up top.

Benny takes his shot, slams it on the table, and then proceeds to drink the other two shots meant for Toya and Nate.

Benny:
What now? Fucking around with me gon have y'all passed out calling Earl. I do this shit!

Nate:
Ok, we drinking drinking, huh?

Nate pours three more shots.

Nate:
You proved your point, cuzzo. I know alcohol kills germs, but quit drinking out my glass. You a savage, so I know you eating Toya butt.

Toya, Nate, and Benny all laugh.

Benny:
Nate, I know yo freak ass ain't talking I shouldn't have drunk out yo glass, nicca. I seen them dirty wide back bitches you be with. Hopefully, this money and that new chain will up your chances of eating some higher quality ass, my nicca.

Nate:
Whateva, nicca!

Benny laughs and does a line of cocaine immediately. He then hands the baggie of coke to Nate. Nate dips his pinky nail in the baggie and sniffs. He then smiles, grabs his shot glass, and raises it up as to toast.

Nate:
Let's toast to family and money, blood being thicker than water. NY to NC mob shit, NICCA!

Benny, Toya, and Nate toast and take their shots of corn liquor as Benny's phone rings. Benny drunkenly fumbles around his bubble vest, trying to find his phone as it rings again. By the fourth ring, he finds his phone and flips it open.

Benny
Yo.

Benny pauses for about eight seconds.

Benny:
Ok, bet. Give me like 20 minutes. I'll be right there.

Benny hangs up the phone and attempts to get up from the table, stumbling a bit.

Nate:
What's good? Who was that? You alright, cuzzo?

Benny:
Yea, I'm good. I gotta run to the spot and grab that. They need a half-cross town on Warren.

Benny takes a few drunken steps and drops his car keys. Toya walks over quickly and grabs the keys off the ground before Benny can grab them.

Toya:
Nicca get in the car. I'm driving since I'm the only one not completely drunk or high.

Benny:
I can drive. I'm good.

Toya:
Yea, yea. Nicca, just get in the car. Besides, it's still the holidays. You know they could have roadblocks anywhere. Just get in the fucking car.

Benny takes another shot of corn.

Benny:
Might as well since you driving. Fuck it.

Nate:
This nicca.

Toya:
Which spot tho?

Benny:
Summer Place.

They all hop in the car and head up the dirt path towards the highway. After about 15 minutes of driving, they pull into Summer Place Apartments and park in front of Building C. Benny attempts to open his car door.

Toya:
Benny, just sit your drunk ass in the car, baby. I got it. I'll run up and be right back. You just need a half, right?

Benny:
Yea, but hurry up. I'm hungry. We gon hit Grace's Seafood after this drop.

Nate:
Hell yea. I need some sweet potato pie right about now in my life.

Toya runs up the stairs, and Benny reaches over and turns up the radio. He begins to sing along to Bell Biv DeVoe's " When Will I See You Smile Again." Suddenly, he notices two cars parked side by side at the building directly across from them. Benny turns the radio down.

Benny:
Those cars look familiar. I seen them before.

Nate:
What you talking bout, cuzzo?

Benny:
Something ain't right. Why they just park there sitting in the car? What the fuck they doing?

Benny leans out the window, squinting through his drunken eyes.

Benny:
I know them niccas! They think they slick. I got something for them muthafuckas. Stay here and keep the car running.

Benny cocks his pistol and tucks it in the waist of his jeans. He then opens the car door and approaches the parked cars slowly and cautiously. He arrives at the first parked car and puts the gun directly in the driver's face.

Apple Corn
Peach Corn

SCENE 11: TEMPERATURES RISING

The boys are parked three cars deep in the parking lot of Beddingfield High School. Vega, Jay, and Dome are sitting around the hood of a green Nissan Sentra. Puff, Cole, Dee, and Smaboo are posted on a grey Chevy Malibu. Maverick, Webber, TKO, and Maverick's cousin Shawn are close by in a Ford Explorer. Two girls approach the group of guys and speak.

Shekia:
They ain't in there. I asked a few people and ain't nobody seen them.

Vega:
Where the fuck them niccas at? We been looking for three days and nothing. They usually everywhere.

Smaboo:
Slug and Keith always be out. You don't think somebody told 'em we lookin' for 'em, do you?

TKO:
Ain't no telling. You know these streets be talking.

Maverick:
It's only a matter of time. They gon show up, and I'mma be ready!

Maverick shows his gun in his left hand. Approximately two-thirds of the boys start pulling out pistols in a show of solidarity. The other girl speaks.

Aaliyah:
Damn, you think y'all brought enough guns? Shit!

Shekia:
I know y'all mobbin' and whatnot, but ain't none of y'all really killers. All y'all either in college or working 9 to 5s. Y'all practically outstanding citizens and junk.

Dee:
We ain't start this shit. That's them niccas. You know we ain't neva scared to throw hands, but you gotta be prepared for anything.

Cole:
Sho'nuff.

Puff:
Hey, it looks like the game letting out. What we gon do?

Webber:
You know everybody hit McDonald's on 301 after the game. We might can catch 'em out there.

Vega:
Good idea. Let's go out there. I ain't gon rest till I get them niccas.

The girls walk off as the boys load up the cars and head out of the school parking lot. They speed away car by car, one after the other, with Vega leading the way in the Sentra. They pull into the already packed parking lot and back into spaces side by side, pouring out the cars in unison. Jay speedwalks up towards the entrance door, peeks in, and runs back to the group.

Jay:
Yo, they in there. I just seen 'em!

Vega takes off his shirt, flings it back onto the car, and starts walking towards the door, followed by the rest of the boys, all jumping up and acting noticeably unruly and hyper. Maverick runs past Vega, swings the door open, and notices that Slug and Keith might have caught wind of the commotion and managed to run out the other side of the restaurant.

Maverick:
They in they car. They 'bout to get away!

Dee:
Quick, get back to the cars so we can catch 'em!

The boys all run back out the door and race to the cars just in time to see Slug's Eagle Talon speed off across the parking lot and back onto the highway. They then burst out of the parking lot, following each other in pursuit, but they are so far behind that they get stopped by a light and are forced to wait for vehicles to pass through the intersection. Before the last car can pass by, Vega floors the Sentra and speeds through the red light while the other cars mimic his impulsiveness, but it's too late; their targets are gone.

Vega:
Man fuck!

Dome:
Don't worry about it, yo. We'll get 'em.

Jay:
Pull over at Amaco.

Vega turns left on Martin Luther King and right on Tuskegee then right immediately into the Amaco gas station parking lot. The Grey Malibu and Ford Explorer follow suit. They all hop out of the cars, adrenaline still rushing from the hot pursuit and heated anticipation.

Maverick:
Damn, how you let them get away?!

Vega:
What you want me to do, run the light and smash into somebody? Plus, I don't trust going too fast with this doughnut spare on my back tire. They was in the wind before we could get to Presto.

TKO:
Nicca, them Talons got a little speed on 'em.

Cole:
If I was driving, I woulda hit the Knight Rider super pursuit mode and pune!

They all laugh.

Webber:
What we gon do now?

Dee:
Fuck it. Let's park on the drive and chill. We did enough hunting for three days.

Smaboo:
Somebody take me to the crib. I'm 'bout to call it a night.

Shawn:
Me too.

Cole:
Yea, I'mma go too Slim.

Dee:
Damn, all y'all niccas going in, damn.

Puff:
Well, I'll take them home because I'm done too. I'll see y'all boys tomorrow.

They all exchange handshakes and embraces and part ways. Dee, Vega, and Jay head towards Snowden, followed by Dome, Maverick, and Webber, while the rest of the boys head home. They pull up and park close to the curb, blasting Tribe Called Quest's "Scenario." While hopping out of the car dancing, they all quote Busta Rhymes' part together.

"Watch; as I combine all the juice from the mind
Heel up, wheel up, bring it back, come, rewind
Powerful impact(boom!) from the cannon!"

Dee spots a neighborhood friend coming up towards them.

Dee:
Yo CB! Come here, man!

Jay spots him too and looks towards Vega.

Jay:
Turn on some reggae so CB can get loose.

Vega stops the Tribe's song and turns on Buju Banton's "Wanna Be Loved." CB breaks into his reggae, dancing immediately as the boys cheer him on. Webber, Maverick, and Dome try to mimic CB's moves horribly while Dee, Vega, and Jay laugh and roast them. They play a few more songs until Maverick and Webber decide to leave.

Vega turns to Dee.

Vega:
Yo, we should head to Raleigh. You know Juan got some bitches up there. You know he a whole pimp. He got a couple of strippers we can fuck with.

Jay:
Somebody said women?

Dee:
Cool. Let's go get some huns.

Vega:
Hold on. I should call first. I don't want us to go all the way to Raleigh and he not even be there.

Dee:
Call him.

Vega:
I don't got his number. Hold on. I'm gon call Harlem. He got his number.

Vega dials Harlem's number, and his answering machine comes on. Puff Daddy and Mase's "Been Around the World" plays as a soft, distinct New York accent is heard over the music.

You've reached Harlem, but I'm busy. Talk to me!" Vega dials again but gets the answering machine once more.

Jay:
You know he booed up with Anna, probably making another baby.

Vega:
It's all good. Let's just go to Anna crib, get Juan number, and then we can just shoot to Raleigh. But what car we gon drive? I don't trust this doughnut on this car going all the way there.

Dome:
Yea, and my inspection gone on my truck.

Dee:
We can just go get my sister car. She let me keep her car for the night. I was gonna go see Shell, but I told her we had something to do earlier.

Vega:
Cool. Everybody hop in. I can take Dee to get Patrice car, then we can go to Anna house, get the number from Harlem, drop off my car, and all head to Raleigh. Dome, park your truck in my parking lot, then we can go.

Dome grabs his truck and proceeds to park in front of Vega's apartment while Vega starts the Sentra. Jay and Dee jump inside the car. Dee suddenly opens the car door.

Dee:
Hold on one sec.

Dee jogs over to the middle of the street and begins to piss his whole government name in cursive, and once he gets to the end, he stops pissing briefly. He then runs back to the letter "I" and dots it perfectly.

Vega yells out the window as Dome returns to the car.

Vega:
Nicca, you getting way too good at that.

Dome closes the car door as Dee hops in the back of the car.

Dee:
I'm gon work on doing the last name too one day.

They all laugh and head down Snowden towards Lane Street. They turn on Lane, cross the highway, and park beside Dee's sister's car. Dee and Dome hop out and get in the red Ford Escort, crank up the car, and follow Vega towards Anna's house.

Vega pulls into Anna's driveway, and Dee parks directly behind him. Vega and Jay hop out of the car, go up the steps, and ring the doorbell. After about four minutes, Harlem opens the door and speaks in a stern tone.

Harlem:
What the fuck y'all want, damn? Who that in the other car?

Vega:
We wanted you to answer the phone, nicca. That's Dee and Dome.

Harlem waves at the other car.

Harlem:
Man, I ain't looking at my phone. I was busy.

Jay:
I bet. I see sweat running down your forehead.

Harlem:
Nicca, what y'all want?

Vega:
We need Juan number. We trying to shoot to Raleigh.

Harlem:
I ain't got Juan number on me. It's in my address book, probably in my car at home.

Jay:
Let's go get it.

Harlem:
I ain't 'bout to go all the way home just to get a number.

Vega:
Please, father. *Pleassssse*!

Harlem:
Nicca, I said no.

Jay and Vega (in unison)
Pleassssse!

Vega:
I promise just real quick, and I'll bring you back so you can finish cupcaking.

Harlem:
Alright, man. Shit, one sec, damn.

Vega:
Yes! Thank you, thank you.

Jay:
Thanks, Harlem World.

Vega and Jay go down the steps and head to get in the car.

Dee:
What he say?

Jay:
He coming out. We had to beg that dude to climb up out that pussy.

Moments later, Harlem joins them in the car. Dee backs up out of the driveway and heads towards Harlem's apartment, followed closely by Vega.

SCENE 12: THE PERFECT STORM

Dee pulls into the apartment complex and parks one spot over from Harlem's car. Vega parks in between Dee and Harlem's Ford Taurus. Harlem opens the rear door, gets out of the car, and walks around to the driver's side of his car. He opens the door and leans in to rummage through his belongings. After about five minutes of searching, Harlem emerges from the car and talks over the roof.

Harlem:
It ain't in here. It gotta be upstairs. Give me one second.

Harlem closes the door, hits the alarm, and heads upstairs to his apartment. Vega leans over Jay to talk out the passenger window to Dee, who is also in the driver seat with his window down.

Vega:
Ayo, Dee, when we get to Raleigh, you gotta see the chocolate one Juan got. She so bad she look like Foxy Brown, but she short and thick like Beauty Dior on the flicks.

Dee:
I want that one. I love a short, thick something.

Dome:
'Bout how many of 'em is it?

Vega:
Last time I was up there, it was three. But you know Juan, it might be more or maybe some new chicks, ain't no telling.

Jay:
Either way, I'mma have me some fun.

Suddenly, a voice is heard through the driver's side of Vega's Sentra. Vega and Jay both turn to find a black handgun pointed directly at Vega's face. Vega, in total shock, struggles to make sense of this situation but manages to make out the familiar face.

Jay:
Benny, what you doing?

Benny:
Shut the fuck up. Y'all thought y'all had me, huh?

Vega cautiously speaks with his hands raised slightly, being careful not to move suddenly.

Vega:
Yo, I don't know what you talking 'bout. We ain't here for you. Our homeboy Harlem stay right here. We just waiting for him to come down.

Benny:
Stop lying. Don't no Harlem stay right there. Y'all niccas here to come get me.

Jay:
He telling the tru…

Benny interrupts Jay and points the gun at him.

Benny:
Shut the fuck up, nicca. I'll kill both y'all easy. You know who the fuck I am?

Dee and Dome watch the exchange carefully but are completely unaware of the severity.

Dome:
Who that talking to Vega? It look like they kinda arguing, but I don't know.

Dee:
I can't see either. It look like Jay cousin that showed us that weed a while back.

Dome:
Yea, I think that might be him, but you know Vega good on that one-on-one.

Dee:
Nah, fuck that. I know that's Jay's cousin, but if he fuck with Vega, we jumping that nicca tonight tho. Ain't nobody got no time for no bullshit.

Vega continues pleading to Benny, but nothing seems to work. He looks into his eyes and sees something totally unexplainable. It is like he can see the evil spirit itself laughing inside of Benny's pupils. It is the most evil, sinister sight and feeling he has ever encountered. Time freezes, and Vega begins to think to himself, *Now God? This is how I die? Now? My life jus begun. Is this what Satan looks like, an emotion? Is this what happens just before you die?*

Benny waves the gun at Vega and Jay violently. Dee and Dome see the gun for the first time and now understand that this is more than an argument. This is life and death.

Dee:
Oh shit, that nicca got a gun. We gotta do something.

Dome and Dee both pull out their guns and cock them.

Dome:
Yea, but if we just start shooting, he gonna kill Jay and Vega for sure. What the fuck can we do?

Dee:
I don't know, but hold on one sec.

Benny puts the gun closer to Vega's face.

Benny:
Get out of the car, both of y'all.

Benny pulls Jay and Vega out of the car at gunpoint and motions for Dee and Dome to get out too. Dee and Dome put their guns in their jackets and get out of the car slowly. Benny instructs the Boys to line up next to each other in a row executioner style with their hands up at the rear of the vehicles. Standing about 7 feet from his targets, he begins to spew his madness while pointing the gun from person to person.

Benny:
Yea, y'all thought you had the jump on me, huh? I'mma make an example out of y'all. Show niccas I ain't to be fucked with!

Vega:
I swear we ain't got nothing to do with you.

Benny:
Didn't I tell you to shut the fuck up, lying nicca?!

Benny turns his aim towards Vega and looks like he's about to pull the trigger. Vega braces himself, preparing for the worst. Dee sees this may be his only chance to possibly save Vega and reaches for his gun in his coat pocket. Benny sees Dee's response, turns the gun towards Dee, and starts squeezing, hitting Dee's upper body. Dee manages to get his hand on his gun, but he is only able to return a shot to Benny's lower half. Vega dives towards the back of the Sentra as Benny shoots towards him, narrowly missing, exploding the tail light and putting a couple of holes near the gas tank. At the same time, Dome shoots Benny while Jay runs off toward Harlem's apartment. Dee hits the ground screaming while shots are exchanged between Benny and Dome. Benny falls to the ground and tries to retreat, crawling backwards, while Dome manages to pick up Dee's gun and continue putting his military training to use. Vega runs to Dee, drags him to the Sentra, and attempts to put him in the car.

Vega:
Dee, you gotta help me. Get up! Get in this car!

Dee manages to muster up enough strength to help Vega get him in the car. Vega slams the door, runs around the car, and jumps into the driver's seat. He cranks up the car and slams it into reverse. Vega looks in the rearview mirror as he's backing up and sees Benny on his back, pointing his gun upward while Dome continues forward, shooting with his gun and Dee's. As Vega speeds out of the complex frantically, Dee moans in pain and utters some words jokingly in a deep, country voice.

Dee:
I'm 'bout to go way from here, cuz.

Vega looks over and spots two small holes in Dee's shirt that look to be closer to his friend's stomach area. Brainwashed by all the violent movies he's seen, Vega assumes that if you're shot in the abdomen and there's no violent spewing blood, then you have more time, and your chances of survival are higher. While pushing the Sentra's engine to its limits, Vega runs a red light, passing by the same McDonald's they were just at earlier. His only thoughts were to get his friend to the hospital as fast as he possibly could.

Vega:
Shut up, Dee. You good. You only hit in the stomach. You gon make it.

Dee continues jokingly in his country accent, speaking while managing to let out a slight laugh followed by a painful grunt.

Dee:
Nah, cuz, foreal, I'm bout to go way from here.

Vega speeds through another red light, passing by The Happy Store, where he had the altercation just three days ago.

Vega:
Just chill, Dee. We almost there. Shut up. Just chill.

Dee leans over and reaches to grab Vega's hand. Vega grips Dee's hand with his right hand while steering the Sentra with the left, looking at the road, then looking back at Dee, looking back at the road, then back at Dee. Vega turns hard on Ward, nearly putting the little Nissan on two wheels.

Dee:
Foreal, Vega, I ain't gon make it. Pray with me, cuz.

Vega looks at Dee's quivering lips, noticing a slight purplish-blue tint. Vega was unaware of how much blood Dee actually lost, but he and Dee were both raised Christians and believed that where there are two, God is present and, therefore, can hear their prayers.

Vega:
Ok, Dee.

The boys begin to pray "The Lord's Prayer" together as Vega manages to make a left on Downing, still pushing the Sentra to its limits with no regard for traffic infractions.

Vega and Dee:
Our Father, which art in heaven, hallowed be thy name. Thy Kingdom come. Thy will be done in earth, as it is in heaven. Give us this day our daily bread. And forgive us our trespasses, As we forgive them that trespass against us. And lead us not into temptation, But deliver us from evil. For thine is the kingdom, the power, and the glory, for ever and ever. Amen.

Vega continues praying while ambulance sirens ring out, indicating just how close they are to the hospital.

Vega:
Lord, please forgive Dee for his sins and allow him into your kingdom, in Jesus' name. Please, Lord!

Dee:
Tell my mama I'm sorry and I love her. Tell everyone I love them. I love you, cuz. Tell my family.

Vega:
Stop, Dee. We almost there. You not going anywhere.

Vega almost makes it to the hospital and spots the ambulance. He then flashes his lights and waves the ambulance down. He looks over to Dee and notices that Dee is no longer conscious. As he slams the car in park, he begins to shake Dee and scream his name as tears pour down his face.

Vega:
Deeeeeeeeeee! Deeeee! Wake up! Wake up, nicca!

Vega flings the door open, runs around the front of the car, and rips the passenger door open, grabbing Dee and dragging him out of the car and into his lap on the cold concrete. While holding Dee, crying and shaking, Vega repeats, calling Dee's name.

Vega:
Dee! Dee! Deeeeeeeeeeeeeee!

The paramedics rush over and attempt to pry Dee from Vega's embrace.

1st Paramedic:
Sir, please let us have him. We can help.

Vega yells as he releases Dee and steps back a bit.

Vega:
Is he gone!? Is he dead?!

The other paramedics wheel over a gurney as the first paramedic assesses the situation.

1st Paramedic:
He's lost a lot of blood. He's in critical condition, but he's still alive.

Vega calms slightly but continues to cry as he watches the paramedics lift Dee onto the gurney and push him towards the ambulance. Suddenly, a hand grabs Vega.

Vega, startled, turns and notices a White male dressed in a suit.

White Male:
I'm Detective Hardy. I received the call about the shooting at Summer Place. I'm here to get your statement and piece together this situation.

Vega:
I ain't got time for this! I got to go see about Dee.

Detective Hardy:
I don't think you understand. Benny said you and your friends were there to rob him, and you shot him.

Vega: (noticeably angry and upset)
That's bullshit, I don't even own a gun. He ran up on us.

Detective Hardy:
Easy kid, calm down. I hear you, but you're gonna have to come with me downtown and take a gun residue test to prove your statement. I personally believe you because once I pulled Benjamin's name in the system, it pulled up a long record of crimes from here to New York, and you and your friends don't have anything other than minor traffic tickets. Not saying you're squeaky clean, but you obviously ran into a monster.

Vega:
I'll do whatever you need me to do, but I need to get to Dee. I gotta call his family. I gotta call my mom.

Detective Hardy:
The sooner we get this over, the sooner I can let you get to your family. But if you're telling the truth and this test comes back negative, it will help your story.

Vega gets in the car with the detective, and they head downtown to the police station. As they drive, Vega struggles to hold back tears, still in shock and disbelief, drowning in fear of Dee's uncertainty. They pull up to the station and park near the rear of the building. While walking to the door, they pass by two officers mumbling and looking at Vega with judging eyes as if they'd already assumed he was guilty. Detective Hardy leads Vega to a small room and instructs him to sit down at the table. Vega complies and sits at the table, noticeably shaking and disoriented. The detective leaves the room for a few minutes and returns with gloves on his hands and a small box. He explains to Vega how a gun residue test works as he performs the procedure.

Detective Hardy:
See, Vega, when a gun is fired, it releases lead and other chemicals that end up in the hands of the shooter. So, if this test comes back negative, then that will be evidence that we can use to discredit Benjamin's story.

Vega remains quiet, still distracted by the thoughts of his cousin.

Vega:
Is Dee alive? Can I go now?

Suddenly, another detective enters the room and speaks.

2nd Detective:
Don't worry about that right now, come with me.

Vega looks confused but gets up from the table and follows the detective out the door.

2nd Detective:
I'm Detective Batts. I got a few questions for you. Get in the car.

Detective Batts opens up the car door, and two other detectives are already sitting in the unmarked Crown Victoria with the engine running, one in the passenger side and the other in the back seat. Vega gets in the car, and Detective Batts slams the car door behind Vega. They pull off on Douglas Street and cross over onto Herring Ave. The car is completely quiet as Vega continues to struggle, holding back tears, trying to be tough but noticeably scared and alone in a car with strangers who seem not to care. The car makes a right on Ward Blvd., and Vega realizes that they are headed back to the Summer Place Apartments. The detective turns into the complex but parks away from the police vehicles and ambulance parked by the roped-off scene that he had just left.

The detective beside Vega speaks.

3rd Detective:
We know you shot him. Your friend is probably gonna die because you out here trying to rob people.

Vega: (puzzled)
What are you talking about?

4th Detective:
Where you put the gun? Tell us the truth!

Vega begins to cry in anger and confusion.

Vega:
I ain't have a gun!. That dude ran up on us! Why are you doing this!?

Detective Batts:
It's the same story over and over, up and down Hwy 95. You got dealers from up north with family and country cousins flooding these small towns with weight and young dumb niccas like you and your friends getting caught up in this whole system. I can look at you and see you not built for this life. You a student at A and T. A fucking college student. Shit makes me sick to my stomach. You got a little more than you asked for, didn't you, Nino Brown? Look at you crying like a bitch.

3rd Detective:
You might as well tell us everything.

Vega sits there, silently sobbing for a moment.

Vega:
I ain't do nothing.

4th Detective:
Take this baby home.

Detective Batts shifts the car into drive and leaves Summer Place. They pull into Vega's grandmother's driveway and park.

Detective Batts:
This ain't over. Now get the fuck out.

Detective Batts unlocks the car door, and Vega hops out and rushes towards the already open door. Vega's mom, Paula, embraces him at the doorway while his grandmother, grandfather, and little sister stand in the living room waiting.

Paula:
It's ok, baby. I got you.

Vega:
Ma, is Dee ok?

Paula:
They had to airlift him in the helicopter to Greenville. Your sister Lynn and Dee's family are already there.

Vega's grandmother, Minnie, comes over to the kitchen.

Minnie:
It's gonna be alright, Vega. You need to go to the bathroom and wash that blood off you.

Vega nods, walks past his little sister, and goes into the bathroom. He turns on the light, runs the water, and lathers his hands, watching the white soap turn burgundy. He then looks into the mirror, sees his eyes red from tears, and puts his head down. He finishes rinsing his hands and dries in a towel when he hears the phone ring from the living room. He heads into the living room as his mom answers the phone.

Paula:
Hello.

She pauses.

Paula:
Hold on one second, Lynn.

Paula motions to Vega to come get the phone.

Paula:
It's Lynn.

Vega rushes over and grabs the phone.

Vega:
Lynn, is he ok?

Lynn:
He's still alive, but it ain't looking good. They said he lost a lot of blood.

They both pause as Vega listens carefully, hearing all the background noises of the hospital. Suddenly, a female screams, and the screams are joined by other screams and crying.

Lynn starts crying.

Lynn:
Vega, he ain't make it.

Vega drops the phone and falls to the floor, crying and screaming in agony. Paula comforts him, crying herself as his little sister and grandmother cry also.

Some time goes by as the house is mostly silent aside from whimpers and a tv playing in the background. It's like time stood still for an hour or two. Suddenly the phone rings and Vega's grandmother answers.

Minnie:
Vega it's for you.

Vega gathers himself, wiping tears and reaches for the phone.

Vega:
Hello.

Voice over the phone:
You know what we gotta do.

Vega:
Come scoop me. I'll be outside.

NC A&T SU

ABOUT THE AUTHOR

Anthony Hilliard Jr. is a North Carolina storyteller with an intimate, firsthand perspective on Southern life. His work blends street realism, regional culture, and cinematic storytelling. Drawing inspiration from true events and lived experience, Hilliard captures the unseen moments of small-town America—stories shaped along I-95's relentless route from the notorious North to the darker Southern corridors. Right Off 95 marks his debut novel.

YELLOWSTONE

STAY CONNECTED

Email:
Vicvegasoulrap@gmail.com

Instagram:
@V8ga252

Facebook:
@anthonyis.vicvega

Donations & Support
Cash app: $V8ga

www.ingramcontent.com/pod-product-compliance
Lightning Source LLC
LaVergne TN
LVHW020512100826
845148LV00003B/768

* 9 7 9 8 2 1 8 9 3 9 2 1 2 *